A Day in the Life of

peanut & Bosco

THE BROTHERS MINOR

A Day in the Life of
peanut & Bosco

THE BROTHERS MINOR

FOR MACIE

As daylight breaks through curtains drawn tight,
Peanut's eyelids open with wondrous delight.
Filled with excitement for the day ahead,
She turns to her friend at the foot of her bed.

"We'll start with a really fantastic buffet.
Breakfast is the most important meal of the day.
Eat up now. It will help us grow strong.
Once we're done we can play all day long."

"I wonder, where should we go today?
There are just so many options to weigh."
With that thought, her imagination ran wild.
As it came to her, she suddenly smiled.

"Together we'll sail the ocean blue.
Let's get our gear and gather our crew.
I'll be the captain and you'll be first mate.
For we be pirates now, sailing a dangerous strait."

"We'll go in search of high adventure,
Hoping we'll find buried treasure.
Avast ye sea dog! Don't complain!
Or Davy Jones' Locker shall be yer bane!"

"Vigilant at night and alert by day,
It is our duty to keep villains at bay.
Over the city we've sworn to protect...
Hark! A crime is afoot, I do detect!"

Answering a call in time of need,
Our heroes react with lightning speed.
Arriving just in the nick of time,
This brave duo thwarts a dastardly crime.

"Now let's swim deep into the sea.
To a realm beautiful as can be.
Deep below, the world above fades.
Behold the kingdom of the mermaids!"

"We move with such ease and grace,
Swimming and dancing all over the place.
Life under the sea is truly carefree.
To be a mermaid is the life for me."

"Into the reaches of space we'll explore.
Far from Earth, we can see it no more.
Here we are surrounded only by stars,
Until we land and touch down on Mars."

"A curious creature looks at us with alarm.
Greetings from Earth! We mean you no harm!
Slowly the alien extends its hand.
Now we made a friend in a strange new land."

"Back now to a medieval land of old.
An age of heroes, brave and bold.
Where knights save damsels and ride trusty steeds.
Many legends abound of their noble deeds."

"Locked in a tower, dreadful and dark.
My fears float away with my hero's bark.
Beware! A fearsome dragon guards the way!
Bosco, my champion, will save the day."

"Let's go back to a time long past.
Where creatures loomed large and vast.
You'll shiver in fear when you hear them roar.
This land is ruled by the dinosaur."

"Where I roam, the ground will quake.
All below me will fear me and shake.
I'm the biggest of the big; a terrible beast.
None tangle with me, not in the least."

"Riding with you is always the best.
Saddle up, boy! We're heading out West!
Riding and ranching — adventure is near!
Time to explore the open frontier."

"So much beauty to see on the plains,
Enjoying the sunset and watching the trains.
Here on the range where the buffalo roam,
There's no better place for us to call home."

"I guess we can't have fun all day.
Time for work and then back to play.
We can do this. Here's the trick.
Let's work together so we finish quick!"

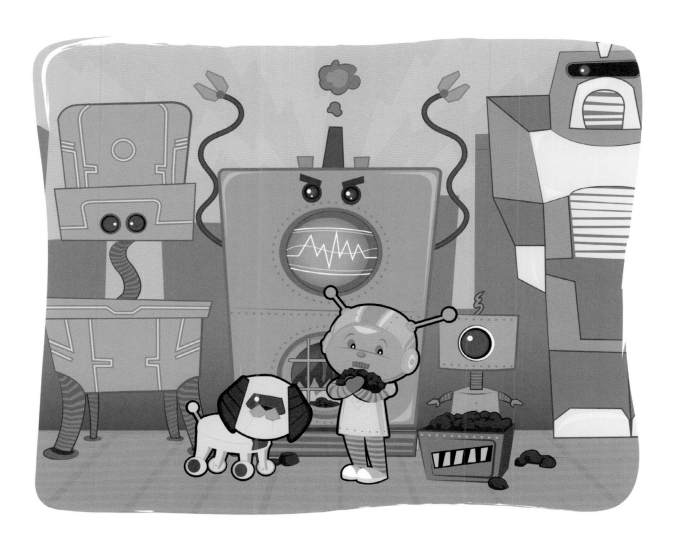

"Sort, stack, fold, and repeat.
Robots work hard! I sure am beat.
Five, four, three, two, one!
Let's go buddy! Now we're all done!"

"Red, yellow, green, and a touch of blue.
Here's a masterpiece, just for you!
Like a witch mixing her brew,
This is a special potion tried and true."

"With this mix I have a fiendish notion.
This here be a wicked potion.
Stir and simmer, the cauldron will bubble...
Magic abound, let's stir up trouble!"

Back at their home with adventure still in their head
Peanut and Bosco get ready for bed.

"What a great day! Wasn't it, pal?
Hope you had fun with your favorite gal."
Where her imagination wanders, they never know.
But that's just a day in the life of Peanut and Bosco.

The End.

Illustrated by Jake Minor
Written by Jake Minor and Kevin Minor
Art Direction and layout by Jake Minor and Danielle D. Farmer
Cover layout by Jake Minor and Brenda McCallum
Type set in KG The Last Time/Good Dog Plain/Comic Sans MS

ISBN: 978-0-7643-5607-0
Printed in China

Published by Schiffer Publishing, Ltd.
4880 Lower Valley Road
Atglen, PA 19310
Phone: (610) 593-1777; Fax: (610) 593-2002
E-mail: Info@schifferbooks.com
Web: www.schifferbooks.com

For our complete selection of fine books on this and related subjects, please visit our website at www. schifferbooks.com. You may also write for a free catalog.

Schiffer Publishing's titles are available at special discounts for bulk purchases for sales promotions or premiums. Special editions, including personalized covers, corporate imprints, and excerpts, can be created in large quantities for special needs. For more information, contact the publisher.

We are always looking for people to write books on new and related subjects. If you have an idea for a book, please contact us at proposals@schifferbooks.com.

OTHER SCHIFFER BOOKS ON RELATED SUBJECTS:

Gruel Snarl Draws a Wild Zugthing by Jeff Jantz, ISBN: 978-0-7643-5397-0

I Am Not a Princess! by Bethany Burt, ISBN: 978-0-7643-5212-6

I Hate Picture Books! by Timothy Young, ISBN: 978-0-7643-4387-2